W9-AXB-303

Summer of
the White Goat

BOOKS BY PAIGE DIXON

LION ON THE MOUNTAIN
SILVER WOLF
THE YOUNG GRIZZLY
MAY I CROSS YOUR GOLDEN RIVER?
PROMISES TO KEEP
THE SEARCH FOR CHARLIE
PIMM'S CUP FOR EVERYBODY

Summer of the White Goat

by Paige Dixon

ILLUSTRATED BY

Grambs Miller

ATHENEUM · *New York*

1977

For Cliff and Patty
who love Montana

Library of Congress Cataloging in Publication Data

Dixon, Paige.
Summer of the white goat.

SUMMARY: A young man observes a mountain goat living
within the boundaries of Glacier Park in Montana as it
deals with the various problems of survival.
1. Rocky Mountain goat—Legends and stories.
[1. Rocky Mountain goat—Fiction.   2. Glacier National
Park—Fiction]   I. Miller, Grambs.   II. Title.
PZ10.3.D6454Su   [Fic]   76–25848
ISBN 0–689–30552–4

Published simultaneously in Canada by
McClelland & Stewart, Ltd.
Manufactured in the United States of America by
The Book Press, Brattleboro, Vermont
Designed by Mary M. Ahern
First Edition

NOTE : I have taken liberties with the fact that no people, not even scientists and naturalists with worthy aims, are allowed to tag or mark the goats in Glacier National Park, although they do so in the neighboring Bitterroot and Sapphire Mountains and the Swan Range.

Summer of
the White Goat

1

THE mountain goat stood on a narrow outcrop of Almost-A-Dog Mountain in the Rocky Mountains of Montana. She had been there for several hours, never moving. Far down in the canyon, a snowplow labored to clear a road. Still further away, men looking small in the distance were blasting to knock down the snow that towered above them.

On an opposite mountain, a billy goat, on a crag hardly big enough to hold him, was silhouetted against pale sky. As an echoing blast of the dynamite rolled through the mountains, the billy goat made a leisurely jump to another ledge, and then sailed up again and disappeared from view.

The mountains were full of sound. Air currents whistled around the nanny goat's head. Not far away a layer of snow broke free of the mountain with a large cracking sound and slid with a rush down the mountain. A boom of dynamite echoed in the thin air. And all around her there were sounds of water: the drip of snow melting, the clatter of streams starting their downward plunge, waterfalls released from ice. It was spring in the mountains.

The nanny goat sought out the place she had chosen, a deep niche in the rocks, at some distance from the band of goats that grazed down below. Here she could be alone. She lay down, finally, tucking her square hooves beneath her, and waited.

In the early afternoon it began to rain. She hated rain. Hunching back as far as she could under the overhang of the rocks, she tucked her feet even more tightly under her. Occasionally she gave her head an impatient shake to throw off the raindrops that caught in her guard hairs. Her coat had begun to shed, and she looked ragged in the front.

Earlier in the day, she had eaten well of purple milk vetch and wheat grass and green lilies, a welcome change after the moss and lichen, the juniper and willow and aspen, of her winter fare.

When the rain stopped, she moved her head forward a little, and with her large amber eyes studied the rocks. There was no sign of other animals. There had been a band of mountain sheep below in the meadow, but they had moved off when the herd of goats came. They wouldn't be back.

It was almost dawn of the next day when the mountain goat gave birth to a male kid. The mother licked him all over to dry him off so the night wind wouldn't chill him. After a few minutes the kid struggled to his feet and began to nurse. On his small head there were two black buttons that would some day grow into horns.

After a short time he pushed his way out of the shelter, and on wobbly legs climbed an overhanging rock. He stood there wavering as the first rays of the sun touched the peaks around them. Then he jumped, but his legs were not strong enough to hold him, and he sprawled in a woolly heap at his mother's feet.

But soon he was jumping again and butting his head against his mother. She stood patiently letting him play. Every now and then the kid let out a sharp little bleat, and the mother answered with a soft grunt. Later in the morning, the kid fed again and then fell asleep. The nanny kept watch, although nothing threatened except an eagle, who circled a few times high above them and then flew away.

When the kid was four days old, the mother began a slow, careful descent to an alpine meadow where food was plentiful. The little goat had already begun to nibble at whatever vegetation he could find.

He was steadier on his feet now, and he liked to dash ahead of her, right to the edge of a cliff, where he would stand and gaze solemnly at the immense depth of space below him. Unlike his mother, he wouldn't stand still for any length of time. And he

still couldn't jump very far. When they came to steep rock faces that the kid couldn't climb, his mother would come back and sniff at him and steer him away to an easier route.

Once when a large hawk circled above their heads, the little goat bleated and ran underneath his mother for protection. She stood still, staring steadily at the bird until it flew away. Then with her strong front legs she boosted herself up the next ledge and waited while the little goat, after several futile attempts, managed to scramble up after her. Their route eventually led down into a meadow still covered with snow, where other female goats and kids and a few yearlings ate steadily of the alpine sorrel that grew around the edge. The other goats glanced at the newcomers without interest, and in a few minutes the kids had discovered each other and were playing, circling and butting and tumbling over each other. The little goat who had just arrived found a narrow, snow-covered gully where he could slide. In a few minutes all the kids were gathered at the slide, chasing each other down the slope.

Some distance away from the meadow in a flat area was a small chalet, snowbound and empty. Late in the afternoon someone on snowshoes struggled up the path to the chalet and set down his pack. In a little while, smoke came out of the chimney.

The mother goats, feeding and keeping close watch over their young, saw the newcomer and noticed the smoke. After a while the newly arrived nanny took up a position on a rock where she could see the chalet and also keep an eye on her kid. Tired from his play, and hungry, he staggered over to her, nursed, and settled against her for a nap. Down in the hollow nothing moved except the wavering column of smoke.

2

INSIDE the little chalet, Gordon Mohlen washed up after his supper of freeze-dried food and sat down facing his small cassette-recorder. He cleared his throat and pushed the RECORD button. Speaking slowly, and occasionally stumbling over a word, he said, "Field Report on Mountain Goats, Habits, Habitat, Behavior. For Mr. Rankin's Advanced Biology, Grade 12, Stevens High School. By Gordon Mohlen, Grade 12." He shut off the recorder and played it back. He erased it and recorded the same words again, making his voice deeper. He went on. "First day of field trip. Arrived by bus and then by snowshoe to chalet designated in permission given by Forest Service to make this study. Cooked supper. On way in, observed several goats, females and kids, in alpine meadow about a quarter mile up and to the west of this place. Caught glimpse of very young-looking kids playing on snowslide. All goats now out of sight except one nanny . . ." He shut off the recorder, picked up his binoculars, and went to the window. After staring through the glasses for a few minutes, he went on with his report. ". . . one nanny may be acting as lookout, perched on rock."

He went outside, and as he came out the door, the goat rose in a leisurely way, planted her front feet on the almost perpendicular rock face behind her, hunched up, and climbed it and disappeared.

Although the mountain wind cut his face and chilled his feet in their heavy climbing boots, Gordon Mohlen stood perfectly still for some time, his hands thrust deep in the pockets of his fleece-lined parka.

After a long wait, the goat reappeared on the same rock. She looked steadily at the chalet, saw nothing moving, and settled into her watching position again.

For another ten minutes Gordon stood still. He noticed that she sometimes lifted her head and made a slow survey of the land below her, but always her gaze came back to the chalet.

When the cold became too acute, he stamped his feet and flapped his arms. At once she was gone. He went inside, and when he had warmed up, he turned on the recorder again.

"Went outside to observe goat. As soon as I appeared, she left, scrambling up sheer rock. Did not act frightened or panicky. Eventually came back, and as long as I stood still, paid no attention to me. As soon as I moved, she was gone again. Obviously not alarmed by stationery objects, but cautious about moving objects below her. Never saw her look up." He played the tape back, listening critically to his own matter-of-fact voice. His feelings were quite different from the sound of his voice. He was excited and thrilled. But Mr. Rankin liked everything to be cool and scientific.

He tidied up the fire, brushed his teeth, spread out his sleeping bag, and was sound asleep as soon as he lay down.

3

Sometimes other goats kept the watch, but always one of them was there. They were not especially alarmed by the young man in the chalet. They had grown accustomed to people appearing and disappearing below them during the spring and summer months. Because they were in a national park, they were not hunted, and so they had not learned to be wary of man. Still, they kept track. If it had not been that their meadow held good and nourishing food, welcome after the harsh winter, they might have moved farther up, as the billy goats did. But while their young were still awkward in their leaping, sometimes careless of danger, and ravenously hungry, they stayed where they were.

More snow melted every day, although even at the height of summer it would not be entirely gone. The goats found tasty meals of huckleberry, horsetail, snowbush. The wool the nannies had begun to shed caught on the bushes, looking like another kind of snow. Their summer coats were coming in with a slightly yellowish tint. The snow was trampled by the inverted V of their big feet with the convex pads that gave them their traction on the rocks.

In the mornings they rose, usually before sunrise, and ate slowly until mid-morning. Then they lay down and chewed their cuds and gazed serenely into space, as their young leaped and tumbled around them. In mid-afternoon they began another meal that lasted until sunset. As the days grew hotter, they looked for shade or lay down in the snow.

One day the goat that had kept close watch on Gordon Mohlen sauntered across the meadow with her stiff-legged walk, looking for her kid. He was alone, very near the edge of the cliff. A shadow fell across the mother's face and was gone. With a loud grunt she ran toward her kid in a stiff-legged gallop. He looked at her and bleated. Then instinctively he dashed toward her and tumbled at her feet. The golden eagle, whose shadow had alarmed the nanny, dipped and then climbed, frustrated in his attempt to capture the kid.

Later that day another kid, also venturing close to the edge of the cliff, was not so lucky. The eagle swooped down and caught him in his great talons and flew away. The nanny kept a close watch on her own kid for a long time after that. Sometimes he tried to run away from her, because he was ad-

venturous and he liked to explore, but she followed him, and when he got tired, he was glad to come back to her and rub up against her for warmth and protection.

He was growing fast. Already he kept his balance better, had learned to climb more sure-footedly, and more often his leaps took him where he meant to go. He was developing the sense of balance that a mountain goat needs to survive. Still, he didn't stray far without his mother's leadership.

He was learning to watch for enemies from below: the occasional mountain lion, bobcat, bear, or coyote. Like his mother, he watched closely anything below him that moved. He seldom looked up, except for bird shadows, because there were no predators who could climb higher than he could. Except, of course, man, whom he had not learned to fear.

But there were times when he was having too much fun to watch at all. One morning, in a mood for adventure, he bounded ahead of his mother, out of the meadow and up the far cliff. In the first jump he didn't allow for enough space from solid ground to the first ledge and fell back in a sprawling heap, bleating indignantly. His mother nosed him and poked him to make sure he was unhurt. He staggered to his feet and made another try. This time he made it.

His mother followed close at his heels as he climbed. Once she boosted him with her head to get him up over a difficult stretch of cliff.

They came, after a bit, to a small level area, a hollow in which icy granules of snow were tightly packed. The hollow was in shadow, on the north side of the mountain. The little goat romped, slipping and falling in the snow, getting up and bounding off again. His mother plodded after him with her slow patient gait, until they reached the far side of the hollow. Above them on a flat rock, a camera recorded their activities, but neither goat ever looked up.

Toward noon the little goat grew tired. He flopped down beside his mother and went immediately to sleep. She sat beside him, her serene gaze taking in the mountains and valleys around her. A sudden snow squall struck, and she bent her head and drew into herself, shaking off wetness every few minutes. Then the snow stopped as suddenly as it began. Down at the timber line, the stunted trees gleamed dull white. The little goat woke, hungry again, and they crossed the meadow, leaped down the cliffside, and came home to their own meadow.

4

GORDON MOHLEN'S hands were scratched and cut and shaking with fatigue, but he turned to the recorder as soon as he had drunk the last of the hot cocoa from his thermos.

His voice trembled with excitement. "Day six. Wonderful luck today. Spent three hours climbing the west face of the mountain only to find I couldn't see the goats' meadow from where I was. Was trying to figure out how to get closer without being seen—the trick being to stay above them all the time—when all of a sudden here comes my own favorite goat . . ." He paused and rewound the tape briefly, erasing "my favorite goat . . ." That didn't sound scientific. "Suddenly there were the nanny and the kid that I've been especially studying. First the kid came, scrambling up the sheer rock to this little hollow right below me. Then his mother came just behind him, giving him a kind of shove over the edge. He sprawled in the snow and looked surprised." He stopped to erase "and looked surprised." He could hear in his mind Mr. Rankin's ironic voice saying, "And tell us, Mohlen, what does a surprised goat look like?"

He went on. "I had the camera set with the telephoto lens, so I had to change the focus fast, because they were not all that far away." He pushed the pause button and tried to get his thoughts organized. "At first I'm sure they didn't know I was there. The wind was blowing toward me, so they wouldn't have got the smell, and they just never looked up. I took a million pictures . . ." He erased the sentence. "I took five rolls of film between about seven thirty A.M. and eleven twenty A.M. I didn't get any shots of them coming up into the hollow, because of my wrong setting, but as soon as they were in full view I took pictures of them browsing, of the kid rolling around in the snow. The nanny mostly watched him and kept her eye on things below her." He pushed the pause button again and consulted his notes. "As we know, the mountain goat is known by the scientific name of *Oreamnos Americana*, commonly called Rocky Mountain Goat or White Goat, of the family Bovidae, which includes cattle, sheep, and goats. But actually the mountain goat is closer to an antelope than to our domestic goat, in spite of certain similarities, such as the shape of the head, the beard, etc. Judging by the goats under my observation this morning, the female is around 150 to 180 pounds, which must make her about twice the size of a domestic goat. The billies I've seen in the distance, with my binoculars, are, I think, a good deal bigger than that, maybe another hundred pounds."

Trying to keep his excitement in check, he went on to describe in detail all that he had seen that morning. He told about the sudden snow squall. He wanted to tell how cold and uncomfortable he had been, so Mr. Rankin would know what he was going through in the name of science, but he left it out. It didn't belong in a scientific report, he told himself sternly. But, man, it had been really cold and wet! And it was his impression that the goat had disliked it as much as he had. He mentioned how she had shaken herself hard every few minutes.

"When the storm ended, she got the kid on his feet and maneuvered him toward the cliff. He got the idea, although he was kind of sleepy." He wished he could describe how cute the little goat was, but that would never do. "Just before she started down the cliff, the nanny turned and looked straight at me. I don't know how long she knew I was there. I had hardly moved all that time, so I guess she wasn't scared of me. It was a funny look . . ." He erased that and thought, But it *was* a funny look, as if she was laughing at me. As if she was saying, "Ha, ha, you big dope, you didn't

fool me. I knew you were there all the time."
He added details about the approximate size and
weight of the kid, the condition of his coat, the
thickness of the legs that were already looking
sturdy. And then the report was done for the day.

He shut off the recorder and turned on the radio.
Very faintly he could hear country-western on a
Kalispell station. He stirred up the fire, made some
more hot chocolate, and opened a can of beans.
Tomorrow he'd have to walk out and get some more
grub. He was running low.

That night, snug in his bedroll beside the fire, he
lay awake thinking about his goats. One of the
things he was supposed to do if possible was to
mark some of the goats so they could be kept track
of. He had some radio collars and some ear tags
and black dye. But he hadn't yet worked out a way
to catch them so he could put the tracking devices
to work. First he was going to have to spend a
long time getting to know their habits. He had it in
his mind to try trapping them with clover but
wasn't sure it would work.

He yawned and turned over as the fire died down.
"Good night, goat," he said. He was thinking of
the one he called his goat. "See you later."

THE GOATS knew that the boy in the chalet had
gone, but after a few days he came back again, and
there was a little stir of uneasiness. They were not
really afraid of him, but he was an unknown factor

to be taken into consideration. The goat Gordon thought of as his watched him hike up the trail to the chalet, his back bent under a heavy pack. It was evening when he arrived, and the last colors of the sunset were just fading from the sky. To the west the mountains still had a faintly pink look. The day had been warm.

He dumped his pack inside the chalet and came out again with binoculars. He smiled as he saw the goat standing at the edge of the meadow. "Hi," he said. "Nice to see you." He went inside and built up the fire. He was hungry and tired.

When he had eaten and washed up, he spread out the contents of his pack. A lot of it was food, but some of it had to do with the traps he hoped to set for the goats. He wasn't too happy about the idea of trapping them, but he wasn't going to hurt them, just measure them and identify them and let them go. He'd talked briefly by phone with Mr. Rankin while he was in the store, and Mr. Rankin had sounded enthusiastic, unusually so for him.

"Get them collared and marked, Mohlen," he'd said. "Be sure you do that. Then we can really get some valuable information."

Gordon planned to major in wildlife management at the university. Maybe this study would help him out, get him a scholarship or something. Not too awfully much had been done on Rocky Mountain goats.

He slept soundly that night and woke early,

prepared to find out before the day was over what the goats used for a salt lick. That would be the best place to set up the trap he had in mind.

He made the long difficult climb up the west side of the mountain again, having more trouble than last time because the handholds on the rocks were wet with dew. Once he fell back several feet, and only escaped a worse fall by grabbing a twisted Alpine fir that grew out of a crevice. Fortunately the fir held, and he was able to get his balance again. He had taught himself not to look down, but the mental picture of that long fall flashed through his mind. A guy could get killed, or at best break a leg or fracture his skull. And if a ranger or anybody happened to find him, it would be only by the purest luck. So take it easy, Mohlen, he told himself. Step by step. Remember how the goat tests out a place before she puts her whole weight on it. He concentrated intently on the face of the cliff in front of him.

Above, in the meadow, the goat had heard him fall. She had herded her kid to the other end of the meadow. Some of the nannies looked up from their grazing, listened for a moment, and then went back to eating. They ignored each other most of the time.

The goat crossed the meadow and climbed the east slope. She made a double jump from one impossibly narrow ledge to another almost as small. From here she made several lateral jumps that finally brought her out above the cliff that Gordon

Mohlen was laboriously climbing. She watched him as he slipped, clung, scrambled, and heaved himself upward. She was still looking down at him when he arrived, out of breath and badly scratched, at the place where he had taken pictures the week before. His back was toward her.

She could also see her own kid, under the lip of the cliff, out of range of Gordon's binoculars and camera. She watched the boy adjust his camera, take some pictures, and then sit very still, waiting and watching. A stiff wind came up and ruffled her long white fur. The boy huddled his shoulders deeper into his parka.

When her kid began to wander out into the middle of the meadow, looking for her, she started back. She took the easiest jump down, a long leap and then another leap, until she came to a steep slope that would lead her into the meadow.

The wind howled, and there was a rattle of loose stones tumbling and scraping down the mountainside. She came around a tight bend in the narrow trail and stopped. The face of Gordon Mohlen, sweating with exertion and scratched by rocks, was just below her. For a moment they stared at each other.

"Well, fancy meeting you here," he said. And then as his left-hand grip began to slip, he said, "Oops! Sorry," and he disappeared from sight. She heard the thump as he came to the bottom of the steep decline. Curious, she peered down the rock face. He was sitting down on a wide rock ledge.

"So I'm not as graceful as you are," he shouted up at her. "Don't rub it in. Hey, where's your salt lick?"

But she was gone, making her easy-seeming, breathtaking leaps, back to the meadow where she had left her kid. He rushed up to her and bleated.

Later when it was almost dark, she and some of the other goats led their kids down to the salt lick, some half mile from their meadow. She smelled the scent of the young man, but she paid no attention to it.

That night Gordon recorded the experience. "And there she was, my own goat, and there I was clinging for dear life to rock that was slippery as glass, my camera slung around the back of my neck, no chance for pictures. But we did meet, face to face, or almost, since her face was two or three feet below mine. I said hello and fell off. No mountain goat Gordon Mohlen. I have no doubt she laughed." He would have to edit this tape later. It was getting more and more subjective, but never mind—just get things down. "Later I trailed them to the salt lick. It's on a bare ridge maybe three-quarters of a mile from the meadow and down about half a mile. It was interesting to watch the pecking order. There were five nannies and six kids—somebody up there has twins. The nannies are really not very nice to each other. They shove and stamp their feet and act very irritated. My goat was num-

ber one, numero uno—at least today—I guess I
know how to pick 'em. The others deferred to her,
not as if they were all that fond of her, but because
she seems to have the authority some way. I don't
think she's so very old. Well, maybe I can get hold
of her and take a look. Tomorrow the clover trap."

5

GORDON was up before dawn, working on his clover trap. On the path the goats took to the salt lick, he dumped some clover that he had brought for the purpose from further down the mountain. Using the few available stunted trees, some bushes and poles, he arranged a trap that would be triggered to fall into place when the goat walked up to the clover. It was hard work, and it took him longer than he had expected. He hoped he wasn't scenting up the place too strongly so that they'd never come near it, but there was a hard wind blowing, and toward the end of his work it began to rain. Down below him in a ravine a stream thundered along, and he was startled for a moment by the shrill harsh whistle of a marmot close by him.

When he had finished, he climbed down to the spot he had picked for his observation post. He huddled on the wet ground, pulling his parka up around his ears, and waited.

Hours later he pulled a soggy sandwich out of his pocket and ate it. Why hadn't he thought to bring a thermos of something hot—soup or coffee or something? He'd been in such a hurry to get his trap set up, he'd forgotten his usual routine things. He stirred uncomfortably, trying to get his legs into a less cramped position. Those darned goats. Probably they wouldn't come till evening. He considered going back to the chalet and getting warm and dry and fed and coming back later, but if he did that, it would be just his luck to have them show up while he was gone. Might as well stick it out. He pressed his finger to his upper lip to stifle a sneeze. If he died of pneumonia up here in the wilderness, nobody would know it. All to get some information about a few crazy goats.

But he remembered Mr. Rankin's account of his own summer by himself in the Klondike, studying the big bear. Nearly got himself killed a few times. But now he knew things about the Klondike bear that probably nobody else knew. He thought of David Mech and his study of the wolves on that island in Michigan. At least Gordon's goats weren't dangerous like the bears, or elusive like the wolves. He sneezed, blew his nose, got up and ran in place for a minute. The little black flies were one of his big problems. They got in his ears, in his hair, down his neck. And mosquitoes. He itched in at least forty-nine different places.

He sat down and slapped at himself. The little bottle of Citronella was almost empty. It didn't seem to help a whole lot. He found a Hershey bar in his inside jacket pocket and ate it. Then he was thirsty. Goats or no goats, he had to have a drink. He went to a little stream that poured over rocks in a miniature waterfall, and cupping his hands, he drank the icy water. He also splashed it over his neck and face and arms and legs, shivering but enjoying the slight shock of the cold water.

The sun came out and almost at once the temperature seemed to soar. The ground steamed. The hiding place he had chosen, behind a boulder, was in the direct path of the sunlight. He began to perspire, and the flies and mosquitoes came out now in clouds. Twice more, in desperation, he ran back to the little waterfall and doused his head. He thought of his cousin Peter who was spending his summer as a trainee clerk in an air-conditioned bank.

Eventually, although he would have sworn it couldn't happen, he fell asleep.

When he awoke, the sun had gone behind the highest of the nearby mountains and his hiding place was in shadow. He sat up and looked at his watch. Might as well stick it out, since he'd waited this long.

About forty-five minutes later he thought he heard a faint sound. Holding his breath he waited.

Sure enough, there came the goats, in single file, kids following nannies, heading for the salt lick. His own goat was in the lead. He sat absolutely still.

The nanny came toward his trap. She smelled the fresh clover, stopped, and lowered her head a little. The goats stopped behind her, waiting for her to go on. She stepped a little closer and stopped again. Her tail lifted to a semi-erect position, and Gordon remembered something he had read about goats' tails indicating their emotions: a tail tightly tucked under meant anger, a totally erect tail meant fear, partly erect showed some anxiety. But if that was true, his goat gave no other sign of anxiety. She stepped with her careful, big-footed gait toward the clover. Then she stopped again, just short of the trap. For a long minute she didn't move. Then she turned aside and licked the ground near it. She walked around the trap to the salt lick, looking back once to make sure her kid was following.

The other nannies followed her, except for the last one, who hesitated, and then moved into the trap. Gordon tensed. But something was wrong with the triggering device. The thing didn't work. The goat ate a mouthful of clover and calmly walked out of the trap.

Gordon clutched his head. All that work, all that waiting, for nothing! He made himself wait until the goats had left the salt lick, and then he tore down the trap in frustration.

The goats had changed their feeding place. Having exhausted the supply at their little meadow, they moved on up the range to another open place. For more than three weeks they stayed there, three unusually hot weeks when the sun beat down day after day on the big jagged rocks. One of the advantages of this new feeding place was that there were several large overhangs where shade and snow made cool resting places.

The kids were growing fast. Most of the time they went about their own business, but they never completely wandered away from their mothers. One day there was a ruckus when a yearling arrived in their meadow and tried to attach himself to his mother. She was Gordon's goat. Without hesitation she chased him off, and although he put up resistance at first, circling her and trying to stay with her, she lowered her horns and made herself clear. He left and did not return. Hours later he could be seen on a cliff, making his way up toward the higher ledges where the billies led their solitary lives.

That problem solved, the nanny lumbered over to the depression where the goats took their dust baths. She lay on her back, and wallowed in the dust. Then she wandered to the end of the meadow and jumped straight down to a cleft in the rock. She stood for a moment, and then jumped down again. Up in the meadow her kid looked after her but didn't follow. Instead he trotted after two other kids and began to play with them.

The nanny made one more jump and then crossed a small open space until she came to a mineral spring. She browsed on the green shoots that grew near the spring.

A sharp wind rattled bushes and sent pebbles and small rocks cascading down the slopes. The sky was cloudy, and there was a distant boom of thunder. A jagged shaft of lightning hit a peak nearby, thunder crashed, and a torrent of rain mixed with hail fell as if someone had torn open the clouds. She found a small cave and backed part of the way into it. After a few minutes an avalanche of loosened rock, brush, and mud swept past her, covering with debris the place where she'd been browsing.

Then the storm was over, and a pale sun shone through the scattering clouds. Daintily she stepped through the soggy brush and made her way around the face of the cliff. The wind had died down with the ending of the storm, and it was unusually quiet. She stopped at a slight sound and looked down.

Gordon Mohlen was a short way below her. He looked very wet. Something small flew through the air and struck her in the shoulder. It stung. She shook herself, and a small dart fell to the ground.

Gordon put his hand out to catch hold of the cliff. "It won't hurt you," he called out. "It's just a tranquilizer."

She swung away and leaped up, then leaped again and continued to climb and circle and climb and circle for almost ten minutes. Then, higher up in the mountains than she had been all summer, she collapsed on warm, wet rocks and lost consciousness.

After a while she struggled to her feet and stood unsteadily, lowered her head and shook it. She studied the territory all around her. Then she pivotted around on her hind legs and started back toward the old feeding ground.

Her kid was waiting anxiously as she jumped down into the clearing. He bleated and rubbed against her. Together they found a comfortable place and went to sleep. The others were already asleep.

It was almost midnight when Gordon peered through his binoculars at the meadow. It was bright moonlight, but even so, it was some time before he could identify the sleeping goat. It was really because of the kid that he was sure. It had stopped trotting about anxiously bleating and was pressed up close to the nanny. It had an identifying brown streak in the wool along his back, and in the moonlight, it made a faint shadow.

"So there you are, then." Gordon put down his glasses and leaned wearily against a rock. "I'll never pull that stunt again," he was muttering to himself. "Darned tranquillizer wasn't strong enough. I could have killed you. You could have passed out and fallen off a cliff or something. No more of that stuff. I'll have to think of some other way." Stiffly he got to his feet and headed for the chalet. It had been a bad day.

6

In the morning the goats moved on to a higher place, although there was still plenty of food in the meadow where they had been. Gordon's goat went first, and the other goats at first behaved as if they didn't intend to follow her, but in the end, perhaps from curiosity, they plodded up the steep mountainside, and made the last few leaps to a spot she had chosen. It had once been a cirque, filled with ice-blue water, but that summer it was dry, and there was good grazing in the former lake bed.

They were a long way now from the salt lick they had been using. In the afternoon the goat set out, with her kid at her heels, to look for another. It took some time and it involved going lower down than she wanted to go. Lower levels meant possible danger. But she kept going until she came to a creek bottom just below timberline. Moss and lichens grew along the banks, and close by there was the path of an old snowslide, now thick with moss. Patches of glacial ice lay between gray boulders.

Since there was food here as well as salt, the goat and her kid lingered for a while, although it was farther down the mountain than she liked to be.

Toward evening she turned and started up again. She picked her way through a small canyon, around thickets of stunted trees, over a sloping field of broken rock. The sun disappeared behind a peak, and then reappeared as the goats climbed upward.

A stream hurtled down off a shelf of rock sending up a spray that caught the sun's last rays and turned into a rainbow. Then the sun was gone again, leaving a red-tinged sky.

The goat stopped and looked at the stream. It was necessary either to ford it, or to jump across it, or to leap almost straight up a shelf of rock above them. She was not fond of water, and unless she had to make a jump on level ground, she avoided it. She looked back at her kid and then jumped up.

She moved to make room for the kid, and then jumped again, to a ledge just barely big enough for her four feet tucked together. She stretched her neck and pulled a twig out of the side of the cliff and munched it for a minute. The kid, below her, gave a small impatient bleat.

The third jump took her to a sloping, rock-strewn stretch, with enormous boulders dumped there by some long-ago slide. Again she waited for the kid, and then started off across the rocky stretch, keeping close to the edge of the cliff.

An updraft rattled the loose pebbles and sent some of them cascading down the mountain. Suddenly the goat stopped in her tracks. Some faint movement had alerted her. Almost at the same time, the kid gave a wild bleat of fear and galloped toward his mother.

Almost hidden in the shadows of a big rock, a mountain lion lay, muscles coiled to spring. The tip of its tail lashed back and forth, and it was this movement that had caught the goat's eye.

As the big cat leaped toward the kid, the goat wheeled around, lowered her head, and plunged at the cat with her dagger-sharp horns aimed at his chest.

The cat's great paw raked the goat's shoulder, and he fought to get his teeth into the side of the goat's skull, but the goat dodged the fierce teeth and a second swipe of the paw. Head down, she caught him on her horns and with a tremendous effort of her shoulders, lifted him off his feet. The lion gave a long, high scream of pain and terror. For a second he struggled high in the air, impaled on the sharp black horns. Then the goat threw her head forward, releasing the lion. The toss propelled the lion over the edge of the cliff. He fell, twisting and turning desperately, and landed on his feet on a shelf halfway down the cliff. Then, he lay still,

blood oozing from his wounds.

The goat's shoulder was bleeding, but she went on her unhurried way up the mountain as if nothing had happened. Only once did she stop, to drink long gulps of water from a cold stream. The frightened kid stayed close at her heels.

When she arrived in the meadow, the other goats glanced at her without curiosity and went on feeding. She lay down in the shadows and slept. By late evening the bleeding had stopped. The wound was painful, but it would heal.

At the chalet Gordon Mohlen recorded the fight, which by chance he had seen. His voice was shaky with excitment and awe. "It was incredible," he said. "I was on my way home from a long climb, trying to get some pictures of a billy goat (never did get them), when I happened to spot the nanny and the kid plodding along toward home as if they'd done a day's work and were tired—at least the nanny. The kid never seems to be tired except when he falls asleep. Anyway, I was watching them through the glasses from a facing cliff across the chasm. I never even saw the cougar till he sprang. I think the goat caught on to him maybe a second before he jumped. He aimed at the kid, of course, but that nanny, that I thought couldn't move fast, was in there before he ever landed. The fight was over in seconds. She got him on her horns and pitched him off that cliff as if he was a sack of potatoes. Boy! that cougar's scream I'll be hearing in my dreams for the rest of my life. But the crazy thing is, I think the lion survived. A big ledge broke his fall, and he landed on his feet, just like they say cats do. Then he kind of crumpled up and lay there bleeding. I was so sure he was done for, I was already starting down toward the mountain so I could get up closer on his side and take a look, when he staggered to his feet. He found a cave in the side of the mountain and he crawled into it, leaving a trail of blood all over the place. He may die, of course, but I have a hunch he won't. I'll check up later. Cautiously!

"Mountain goats may be peaceful animals but I'd advise anybody not to get any ideas about having kid for supper if nanny's anywhere around. Man, those horns! And the strength in the shoulders and neck it must have taken to lift that heavy cougar and pitch him off like that! It was real luck that I saw it. You wouldn't see something like that in a million years."

He turned off the recorder and sat reconstructing the scene in his mind. He had had a moment of real fear that his favorite goat was going to be killed. But not she! He had seen blood on her white shoulder, but it hadn't appeared to be bad enough to slow her down any. She was one terrific goat, all right.

7

Because he was concerned about her, Gordon went looking for his goat early the next morning. But first he checked with the glasses from a safe distance to see if the mountain lion had survived. He couldn't see the inside of the dark cave from where he first perched, so he decided to climb to a higher ledge that would bring him almost opposite the cave, where there was a narrower distance between two cliffs. It was a tricky climb. He un-looped the rope he wore around his waist and tossed the end of it over an outcropping of rock above him. In spite of all the climbing he had done, especially this summer, he still had to remind himself not to look down.

Making sure the rope held, he dug the heels of his climbing boots into the tiny crevices in the rock face and pulled himself up to the next ledge. In a few minutes, hot and sweaty and scratched, he had reached his objective. The ledge was just big enough for him to stand on with his back flattened against the rock. The sun was hot, and a cloud of no-see-ums pestered him. Moving slowly and with great care he wiped his sleeve across his eyes and lifted the glasses.

The cave across from him was shallow. It must have been just big enough to hold the cougar. He could see nothing but shadows until a cloud that had obscured the sun obligingly moved and the sunshine streamed into the cave. The back was still dim, but he could make out that it was empty. There was no new trail of blood outside the cave, although he could see yesterday's paw prints in the dried grass on the ledge. For the sake of his report, he made a guess at their size. With the glasses he could plainly see one whole footprint, with the four toe pads set in a curve in front of the big heel pad, the whole thing maybe four inches long, four and a half or four and three-quarters wide. An adult cat, all right and a male. Maybe two hundred pounds or so, though that was just guessing from the way the toes splayed out from the heel pad. It was amazing, the strength of that nanny goat!

He scanned the lower reaches of the mountainside looking for any sign of the lion. He was about to give up when, far down almost to the bottom of the ravine, he saw him. The animal was lying on a rock in shadow, looking almost like a shadow himself. He was looking up, and it seemed to Gordon that he was looking directly at him. The time had come, he decided, to get out of there. He knew mountain lions almost never attacked human beings, and when they did, it was probably because they mistook them for another animal, but it didn't make him want to take any chances.

He gave his rope another upward toss, missed the sturdy little fir tree he was aiming at, tried again, and got it. After testing it carefully to make sure the tree would hold, just to be on the safe side, he gave the rope an extra loop around a rock near the top.

When he was safely on top and could relax again, he took another look at the lion. He was still there, as if he had not moved a muscle.

"Good luck, old cat," Gordon said. "You had a narrow squeak. That'll teach you to lay off goats." He coiled up his rope and trudged across the sloping rock field to look for his goat. She was not in the meadow, and he wandered around, looking for the new salt lick. The idea had come to him that maybe he could make a lariat noose for catching a goat. He'd be on the other end, of course, to make sure she didn't choke. It was worth a try. Time was getting on, and Mr. Rankin was going to have a king-sized fit if Gordon didn't get some goats marked and tagged so they could be checked on later. That was one big aim of the whole project.

Late in the afternoon he came upon the salt lick

by chance. He'd seen some goat tracks in the soft ground near a stream and had followed them. There they were, four nannies and four kids, but Gordon's goat was not among them. He felt a little worried about her. That injured shoulder could be causing trouble. He lay still, concealed in brush, until the goats left the salt lick, and then at a discreet distance he began to follow them up to the meadow again. Maybe by now the nanny would be back from wherever she had gone.

He loitered behind the goats so as not to disturb them. Sometimes he had to find his own way up the mountain, not having their ability to leap up, and in time they got so far ahead of him, he couldn't see or hear them any more. It might be just as well, he decided finally, to call it a day and go back to the cabin to get caught up on his notes. Early in the morning he would come out and rig his lariat trap to see if that would work. If he could just mark two or three goats, get those radio collars on them, he would feel a lot better. As the summer wore on, the goats would move gradually higher and higher, and it would be more and more difficult to keep up with them. He was not, after all, a goat.

Thinking and planning, he went around a switch-back trail that animals had made, and then as he moved past a big rock, where the trail fell off on the other side into a deep chasm, he found himself face to face with his goat. He gasped, and he was sure that she was as surprised as he was. Her kid was right behind her. He had never seen her so close before. It made his hands tingle; it was like having a dream you've had for years that you don't honestly believe in, come true. He had a ridiculous impulse to talk to her. He cleared his throat.

"Good evening," he said.

The goat, who was not more than six feet away, stared at him with her big amber eyes. She showed no sign of alarm except a sharp backwards jerk of her head, which he interpreted as a warning for him not to come any closer. Her nostrils flared to take in his scent. She blinked and refastened her gaze on him, but she did not make any movement to retreat.

"How you feeling?" he asked. "How's . . . uh . . . your wound?" He saw where the shoulder wool had been torn. "You really gave that cougar what-for, didn't you." He had the crazy idea that if he kept talking, she wouldn't go away, and he very much wanted her to stay. His mind was obediently noting the data: the scraggly beard that grew underneath the chin, the thin backward-curving hollow horns with three rings—that meant she was about three and a half years old, because once the horns appeared, their growth stopped for a time each winter when food was scarce, and that was what made the rings. The fine wool coat, maybe four inches thick, a little scraggly now with a few bare patches. Short stumpy legs. Heavy shoulders. He thought of the cougar again and shivered. "You aren't mad at me, though, are you? I'm your friend." Weight maybe one hundred fifty pounds? Big flared ears. Black hooves. Hair longer on withers and haunches, making her look humped. . . .

She lowered her head a little.

"Oh-oh," he said. It occurred to him that neither of them could get past each other on this narrow trail. "I see. I'm in the way. Well, you could turn around and go back, you know. I mean, one of us has to give, right?" He looked past her at the kid, who was close on her heels, staring at him inquisitively. "That's a cute kid you've got there," he said, and giggled. His voice broke, and he knew he was nervous. His voice never cracked any more except when he was nervous.

The goat stamped her feet at him and shook her head slightly.

"Oh. You think I'm the one to turn back, do you? Lord, you've got queenly ways, you have."

She pawed the rock again, stamped imperiously, shook her head. She didn't seem angry, only impatient and . . . the only word he could think of was "bossy."

"All right, if you're going to be that way about it. But it seems to me you're carrying things too far." He looked behind him and backed up, his hand on the cliff beside him. "You needn't think I'm going to turn my back on you, mama. One playful little butt from you, and that would be the end, and I do mean the very end, of Gordon Mohlen,

Boy Scientist. So just cool it, I'll give this round to you, but don't rush me, baby." Slowly and carefully he backed around the curve of the switchback until he came to a place where he could let her pass.

She gave him a long thoughtful look (or was it a blank look? he wondered), and with the kid skittering close at her heels, went on down the trail.

"Well," Gordon said. "Boy meets goat."

8

T<small>HE</small> lariat noose was a failure. The goats simply walked around the camouflaged hole where they should have tripped the rope. When all of the nannies and their kids had calmly bypassed it, Gordon gave up. He was beginning to wonder if he would ever be able to trap a goat, in spite of all his work and his scheming. It was discouraging.

It was time again to go out for supplies, but the evening before he left, he spent hours drawing and discarding different types of traps. Some he had heard about or seen; some he dreamed up himself. They had to be fairly simple, and they had to be made mostly of material that was available.

He decided finally on two alternative plans, one of them a net that would drop over a goat's head and tangle her up long enough for him to mark her and take her measurements. The other one, if the net didn't work, was a pen. It would be a lot of work, he reminded himself, so he would try the net first. He would get some netting while he was out, and use rocks for weights. . . . He marked the drawing carefully. There was a likelihood the sudden entangling would scare the goat, but if he worked fast, it shouldn't be too hard on her. The nannies didn't seem very excitable. He was the one who got too excited.

He left early the next morning for the long hike out.

The nanny watched him go down the mountainside. She had moved again, after the encounter with the mountain lion, circling around to a place from which she could see the chalet, though it was much farther away than the place she had been when Gordon first came. The new spot was above timberline, in a maze of peaks and gullies and small stretches of relatively level land where the goats could graze without being bothered. Food was plentiful now, and would be for another couple of weeks before the killing frosts and the heavy snows set in again.

The goat gave up watching Gordon as he became a smaller and smaller speck on the trail. Way down at the bottom a few cars drove along slowly. The cars in summer were one of the reasons the goats grazed higher in the mountains than they once had. The coming of the roads cut down on the territory that they felt comfortable in.

The kid, who was now taller and heavier, stood beside her, watching. On another trail a big billy goat stood alone, also watching. The billies stayed by themselves most of the time, except in the mating season. In another year the kid would be up there himself on some lonely crag. As a yearling, if he tried to stay with his mother, as some did, he would be driven away, because she would have a new kid to look after.

Almost as if he felt the loneliness of the old billy goat that he was staring at, the kid moved closer to his mother. But it might have been because of a sudden chill in the air. Clouds, not dark enough for thunderheads, had piled up overhead, and the wind had picked up a new zinging sound as it whipped around them and rattled the hills.

The nanny's long hair rippled in the wind, but she took little notice of the change in the weather. Weather in all its extremes was part of her daily life. But when it began to snow, she looked for shelter. She and the kid huddled under one of the few big rocks in the field where they were. Other goats hunted for shelter, but there was not enough for them all. The kids huddled close to their mothers, who stood with their heads down. In a few minutes it was snowing so hard that the goats couldn't see each other in the swirling whiteness. A brief summer blizzard at this altitude was not unusual, but this one was cold and cutting, and the noise of the storm was enough to shut out everything else.

Somewhere not too far above them a single-engine plane fought to get above the storm, but the goats never heard it. And far below them cars were stalled. Some tourists sought the shelter of Gordon's chalet. A Jeep came slowly along the road, driven by a forest ranger, looking for motorists in trouble. But the goats could see none of this, nor could the people see the goats. Everyone was caught in his own tight little world of wind and snow. It went on all afternoon.

Somewhere near the nanny and her kid, another kid took a few exploratory steps toward the edge of the cliff. A drift of snow gave way. The kid gave a wild bleat and fell over the edge. It was not until early evening, when the storm finally cleared, that his mother knew he was gone. She hunted for him all over the meadow, but he was not there. Far below, a ranger in a Jeep saw his body and carried it away. Later he said to another ranger, "I don't know why I didn't just leave him there, poor little devil. What do I do with him now?" He was a young ranger, his first year in the service.

The older ranger smiled. "Give him a good Christian burial, Simms. It's the least you can do." But in spite of his joking tone, he looked at the torn body of the little goat with sadness in his eyes. "We lose a lot of 'em that way, but not usually this early in the year."

And in the settlement where he had gone, Gordon watched the weather and worried about his goat. So much of their wool came out during the summer, they weren't as well equipped for a storm like this as they would be later on. But she was a pretty sensible old goat. She'd probably manage.

On his way back, he stopped at the ranger station and heard about the dead kid. He felt a real stab of alarm, as if some member of his family were in danger. "Do you happen to know if it had brown fur along its backbone?"

"No, pure white, as much as we could tell. He got pretty banged up."

He felt relieved, though he was sorry for whatever kid it was, and for whoever the mother was. A scientist wasn't supposed to get all emotionally involved with his subjects, but Gordon found that he did. Maybe he wasn't cut out to be a scientist, after all. Well, he'd just watch it—keep his feelings under control. It didn't do the little dead goat any good, after all, for him to get all upset about him.

He hitched a ride with a ranger partway back to the chalet, and walked the rest of the way, carrying his heavy pack over the soggy, slushy ground. It was slow going. The sun came out in midmorning and with it came hordes of no-see-ums, a regular convention of insects, as if, Gordon thought, they were celebrating the fact that it wasn't really winter yet after all.

He arrived at the chalet and found traces of the visitors. A fire still burned low in the fireplace, and beer cans were sitting on the table in the kitchen.

He cleaned the place up first of all. Then he got binoculars and went out for a look. He had a pretty good idea where the goats were—he had seen them before he left—though he wasn't sure they were staying there. There she was, though, his own goat, sitting calmly on a rock, surveying the world and chewing her cud, as if there had been no cougar, no storm, no lost kid. That, he thought, is known as keeping your cool.

All right, old girl, tomorrow we try the drop net trick. I give you fair warning.

9

GORDON overslept. When he awoke, he had a bad cold. His nose ran, he sneezed, his head ached, and his bones hurt when he tried to turn over in bed. Oh, no, he thought. I'm not going to make it today. Precious time lost. After a few minutes he tried to make himself get up, but he fell back again, feeling terrible.

He dozed for a while, dreaming frightening dreams of falling into snowy chasms and being attacked by bears and cougars. Once when a dream frightened him awake, he said aloud in disgust, "What a great naturalist!"

In the middle of the morning, thirst drove him to get up. He stumbled over the water bucket, with his sleeping bag wrapped awkwardly around him, and drank a great deal of water. When he splashed some on his perspiring face, without warning he began to shiver. So with a great effort, he stooped down and built up the fire. There was aspirin somewhere in his kit. But where was it? He couldn't seem to manage anything. Then when he did find the box, he dropped the tablets twice before he got two into his mouth, and then they dissolved before he could get a drink from the dipper. They tasted awful. He remembered that he had done the same once when he was a little boy, and he had refused for a long time afterward to take aspirin for anything.

Flopping down on the floor near the fire and pulling the sleeping bag tightly around him, he wished he were home.

When he slept, he dreamed that his mother had brought him some hot soup. But when he woke, he was still there in the cabin and he needed firewood. The people who had used his cabin had burned up some of what he had cut, and he had intended to chop some more this morning. Now he couldn't. He fed the logs he had sparingly into the fireplace, just enough to keep the fire from going out. It would be great if you could shut it off, he thought, like pushing down a thermostat, during the times when his fever made him hot.

He took some more aspirin at noon, drank a lot of water, and made himself eat an orange. Then he slept again. By early evening, he felt a little better. It seemed to him that his fever had gone down some. After easing his last piece of firewood onto the fire, he zipped himself into his parka with the drawstring tightly drawn, got his axe, and went outside. His legs were unsteady and he felt as weak as if he had been ill for months, but he set his Coleman lantern on a stump and dragged some of the smaller logs over to the chopping block. A good thing he had plenty of logs stacked up. All he had to do was split them down to size for the fireplace and gather up some kindling for the stove. Split a few lengths of stove wood, too. He was beginning to feel hungry.

Chopping the wood, usually a task he rather enjoyed, took so much of his strength that he had to lean against a tree, weak and perspiring, in between spells of splitting. What a stupid thing. He must have some kind of flu. Twenty-four hour kind, he hoped. That's what he got by going out and mixing with people. You'd never catch the flu from a mountain goat. Of course if you got too chummy with them, you'd catch their ticks and lice and what not, but they weren't about to let you get that close. He wondered if it was true that parasites often killed the animals. That was why they took those slow, rolling dust baths, on their backs, to get rid of some of the pests. Poor old goats.

He felt light-headed by the time he had enough wood for the night. "Better get it inside, Mohlen," he muttered, "before you fall flat on your face." Gathering up an armful, he went inside with his axe tucked under his arm and his lantern in his hand.

His body felt awfully hot again, but maybe just from the exertion. He shut the door and leaned against it, letting the wood fall to the floor with a series of clunks. It was a full minute before he had caught his breath, and his heart had stopped racing. Man! a guy thought he was in such good shape, but all it took was one invisible little non-filterable virus to knock him out. "Pride goeth . . ."

He could hear a coyote barking somewhere close by. Another one, farther away, answered. Probably out rabbit hunting. He'd seen their tracks in the snow when he came in. He liked coyotes. They were smart. Some rancher down in the Bitterroot had written an angry letter to the paper because his boy told him about a report Gordon had written for science class, defending coyotes. To some of the ranchers, all coyotes were enemies.

Well, never mind the coyotes. Get a fire going in the stove. Eat something. Got to get going tomorrow. The days dwindle down. . . . He made the effort, got the paper and the kindling into the stove, added a couple of sticks with shaved ends to catch the flames. When the fire was going properly, he opened a can of stew, poured it into a pan, and set it heating. He was very hungry and ate another orange while he waited for the stew to heat. In his haste he scorched the stew on the bottom, but it tasted good just the same. Then he poured himself some more water, put some more wood on the fire, and collapsed wearily into the sleeping bag. He slept all night, and when he awoke in the morning, his fever was gone.

Over a big breakfast, to get his strength up, he let himself think of how frightening it would have been if the illness had gone into something serious, like pneumonia, for instance. His mother had a point after all, when she worried about his being up here alone. Maybe if he came up next summer, he'd bring in a citizens' band radio or something.

When he started out with the equipment for the drop net, his goat was up there keeping her watch. No doubt she had her eye on him.

"No fair peeking, old nanny," he said. "I'm going to pull a trick on you."

He took the trail to the salt lick, hoping they hadn't meanwhile found themselves another one. It was a cool, sunny day, with a hint of autumn in the air. His favorite time of year.

He walked and climbed a little more slowly than usual, still a little weak. But at last he reached the place and prepared to set up his trap. There were many footprints in the damp ground and in the snow that still remained: Deer prints; the two-toed print of the pronghorn; and some smaller animals —raccoon, porcupine. Off at one side, in a straight, narrow line in the snow, were the dainty prints of the fox. Gordon hoped he wouldn't catch any of the wrong animals in his net. Some of the more inquisitive ones, like the coon, for instance, just might go barging in uninvited. Well he'd have to chance it, and if they did, he'd free them, but it would mean having to set up the trap again. Maybe he could just scare them off.

In spite of the coolness of the air, he got very hot with the effort of getting the drop net in place, arranging rocks that were to act as weights. In his pack he had a measuring tape, a blindfold, and some caps to put on the horns for safety's sake. There was no point in being gouged as the mountain lion had been.

When everything was ready, he settled down in his blind. The cool breeze kept the insects off, anyway, and the sun on his back felt good. He was almost asleep when a scarcely distinguishable sound made him jerk to attention. At first he couldn't see anything from his blind, but then a varying hare hopped into view. He was a big fellow—at least five pounds, Gordon guessed. The hare's brown coat had not yet begun its change to winter white. As it reached up to nibble at the bark of a woody plant, Gordon could see its reddish-brown throat and white undersides. Its big ears twitched constantly, listening for danger.

For a few seconds Gordon didn't move. Then as the hare hopped toward the trap, he said quietly, "Shoo, rabbit. Take off."

The hare was gone like a shot. Poor things. They had to worry about all kinds of enemies, from ticks to lynx. Gordon settled down again to wait, hoping the goats wouldn't take all day about coming down to the salt lick. As far as he had been abe to discover, they didn't come always at the same time of day, although he had never seen them there in the morning.

The breeze died down, and the sun grew warmer. Gordon felt sleepy. He shifted his position slightly and tried to make himself listen to the many small sounds of the wilderness: the slight whisper of leaves in moving air; the patter of some small animals he couldn't see; the occasional twitter of a bird somewhere further down the mountain; the buzz of an insect; the faint rustle of sliding earth; a plop as melting snow near him fell from a tree.

And then he saw the goat—his goat—leading the parade to the salt lick. She plodded along with her head down, as if her thoughts were miles away. Her kid was behind her, and Gordon was startled to see how much he had grown. Then came the other goats. Gordon crossed his fingers and held his breath.

The nanny walked right up to the trap, and for a second Gordon was tempted to warn her off. She was his goat, and he hated the idea of fooling her. But that was insane! What would Mr. Rankin say to such nonsense? That was what he was here for. Anyway, he wasn't going to hurt her.

But he needn't have worried. She stood stock-still for a few seconds, then turned aside and walked around the trap. Forgetting the reaction he had had a minute before, Gordon was irritated and frustrated. How had she known? Could she smell him? He didn't think so. There was no wind, and goats reportedly weren't so great at smelling out danger. He watched helplessly as the goats who followed her also avoided the trap.

But just as he'd given up hope, the last nanny in the line, one of those without a kid, stepped up to the trap. In a matter of seconds she was kicking

helplessly in a tangle of net. By the time Gordon got to her, the other goats had disappeared.

He caught her from the back and got the caps on her horns and the blindfold around her eyes, but she still thrashed in a panic. He talked to her soothingly as he tried desperately to get her measurements. He had tied her up enough so she couldn't get loose, but it was no cinch trying to measure her length, her girth, her tail, the circumference of her horns, while she struggled.

"Easy, easy, easy. Don't freak out like that. I'm not going to hurt you. Shoulder height three feet. . . ." With one hand he scribbled on the yellow block of paper he'd brought. He couldn't trust his memory. "A little over a hundred pounds . . ." He wished he had some kind of scale. Not that he'd ever be able to hold her on it. Two guys needed for this. "Hold still, darn it." He stretched the tape. "Horns, nine inches. Four growth rings. Guard hair maybe . . . Hold still . . . maybe seven inches. Eight inches of lower leg has no hair." He fumbled one of the radio collars out of his pack with one hand and got it around her neck after a considerable struggle. With the black marker he gave her a quick streak of dye along the rump. Then he slipped the caps from her horns with one hand while he cut the net loose with the other. Slapping her on the flank gently, he said, "Go! I apologize."

For a moment she stood still, trembling violently. Then she leaped forward, crashed through the un-

derbrush, leaped up the nearest ledge, and disappeared.

Gordon sat back and mopped his face. "Wow!
I'll never do that again! The goats would end up
with nervous breakdowns, and so would I. Sorry,
Mr. Rankin."

10

T H E marked goat never went back to the little herd. If it hadn't been for the radio collar, which Gordon used to track her with his mobile antenna, he never would have known what happened to her. She went far up into the mountains, to what would normally be winter range, where she stayed alone, as far as he could tell. He felt guilty about that goat. It would be awful to have some creature swoop down on you and tie you all up in a big net. But he had the measurements, and he would be able to track her during the weekends in the fall, when he came back up here. It would be too bad, though, if she became a neurotic goat. She had turned out to be a lot more high-strung than he had expected. He was glad it hadn't been his goat that he had half scared to death with the trap.

That night he worked on sketches of his pen trap.

If he couldn't work something out that wouldn't scare the goats so much, he would just give up the whole idea, and the heck with Mr. Rankin. But it seemed to him that the pen might work. He sat up late, fooling around with the sketch.

It took him two days to build it. He had to cut tall poles to make the enclosure, and saw smaller pieces to make a frame and a crossbar brace for the door, using his axe and a Sven saw, as well as the larger saw he used for firewood. There was a shovel at the chalet that worked for digging post holes, but it was hard to get down in that rocky soil. His hands were soon blistered and sore. On the second day he took along a supply of Band-Aids and a pair of heavy work gloves. When he finally got the poles up and braced, he had to string wire around the sides of the enclosure and over the door. Using a nail and the door lock that he had borrowed from the door of the chalet, he rigged up a mechanism that he could use to trip the drop door from his blind. As far as he could tell, the only way a goat could break out of the enclosure before he could get to her would be to charge at the place where he had run out of wire and had completed the enclosure with net. But the chances were against her running into that particular spot.

He sat back on his heels outside the trap and looked it all over, feeling rather pleased with himself. It just about had to work. Of course he was going to have to get into that enclosure fast and get that goat blindfolded and horn-capped before she got a chance to charge him, as she well might if she felt cornered. Well, he'd taken his chances with sharp horns plenty of times in roping contests, and he hadn't been cut up yet.

It was late afternoon. Since the pen was finished, he decided to stay there and see what turned up at the salt lick. If he went back to the chalet, which his tired and aching body urged him to do, the goats would have a chance to nose all around the trap and maybe decide they wanted no part of it. Surprise was the element he needed. So he checked the tripping device that would lower the door behind the inquisitive goat, and once more settled down to wait.

The sun had left the area where he sat, and he was cold. This time though, he had brought along his warm sweater to wear under his parka while he waited, and in his pack he had a thermos of hot coffee and some sandwiches. As he sat, he put together in his mind a project he hoped he could manage, if his report on the goats was satisfactory. A university student who had radio-tagged some elk had been given a ride by the Fish and Game Department over the area once a week in a plane that had special antennae on the wings, so he could pick up the elks' frequency and keep track of their winter range. The same thing could be done with the goats. Only first, he had to get them collared. He couldn't see Fish and Game doing it for just one goat.

A little before six o'clock, there came Madame Goat, strolling along with her gang behind her. Gordon poised at the ready, to work the triggered door. She gave the pen a curious stare, but she didn't pause for more than a moment before she marched right on in. Gordon worked fast. If Mama goat got too worried about the kid, she'd be twice as hard to handle. He tripped the mechanism almost as soon as her hind feet were in the pen, and the door dropped shut.

The kid bleated, and the other goats stopped. The nanny never even hesitated. As if she had already mapped the structure of the pen, she trotted straight at the space that was patched with net, lowered her horns, and went right through it. Within one minute all the goats had disappeared, including the nanny, with shreds of torn net hanging from her horns.

Gordon fell back against the tree and flung his arms out wide. "No!" he said. "I don't believe it!" After a minute of despair he got up and surveyed the trap. All that work for nothing. Now the question was, was it worth it to patch it up and try once more, or would they be spooked off the thing forever? Maybe even from the salt lick itself. Why had he ever had this brilliant idea about trapping goats?

He looked at the tear in the net. How had she known? Just pure dumb luck, or did that goat have some extra sense he didn't know about? He leaned against a tree and groaned.

Rather than waste all that time setting up another pen somewhere else, he decided to give this one another try. Probably futile, but it was worth a go. He was pretty sure his own goat wouldn't make the same mistake twice, but one of the others might. He got out the leftover net from his pack and patched the hole, making it double thickness. Which I should have done in the first place, he thought. He would stay out all day tomorrow and see what happened. If it were wolves or bears or foxes, they'd never come near the place again, but then, they probably wouldn't have come in the first place. Goats were not all that suspicious.

He went home and had a hot bath out of a bucket, ate a big dinner, and got caught up on his notes.

Up on the mountain the nanny goat rubbed the last of the annoying net off her horns onto the limbs of a dwarf birch, and then went back to her meadow to have another meal. There was a heavy frost that night. Eating would get less and less easy from now on. She settled down calmly to chew her cud. The incident of the pen had not frightened her. It had startled her for a moment, but since she had been able to get out of it with no real trouble, it hadn't seemed like a threat. She had already forgotten about it.

11

AT ten minutes past four the next afternoon one of the goats walked into the pen and looked around in surprise as the gate dropped shut behind her. In seconds Gordon had swung his legs over the gate and was tying the blindfold around her head and putting the caps on her horns. She made no effort to get up once the blindfold was on. Working quickly and talking in a low soothing voice, he marked the dye on her shoulder and got the radio collar on. He made the measurements rapidly, this time trusting to his memory so he wouldn't have to keep her there long. Then he guided her to the gate, lifted it, slipped off the caps and the blindfold, and let her go. She stood still for a moment as if she were bewildered, then shook her head and walked around the pen to the salt lick as if nothing had happened.

The other goats had not run off. Gordon reset the gate and went back to the blind. Maybe he would luck out and get one more. The whole operation had been so fast and so quiet, none of them had showed any signs of alarm.

His own goat walked around the pen, giving her kid a shove with her nose when he showed signs of curiosity, but she paid no attention to the other goats. Mountain goats, Gordon made a mental note, are not cooperative creatures except when eating together, while the kids are young. He watched intently. Another goat bypassed the pen. But the next one wandered in and began to eat the clover he had left on the ground. He triggered the gate, and tagged, collared, and measured this goat with the same speed and ease. This was getting to be child's play: Kid's play, he thought and almost laughed aloud. He felt jubilant that something was working at last.

Before the goats left the salt lick that night, he got two more. None of them put up any resistance except the last one who tried to pull away, and almost succeeded, as he was putting the blindfold on. That, he noted afterward, was because he was getting overconfident and didn't work fast enough.

He made no attempt to capture any of the kids. That might cause a ruckus with the mother. Once when a kid wandered into the pen, he simply left the gate up until it wandered out again.

He left the pen in place, thinking that maybe he

could get one more. But that would be all. Before he went home, he wanted to try to get closer to some of the billies. It would mean a lot of high climbing, and he knew he'd never be able to trap them, but so far he had seen them only from a distance, and he hadn't gotten any really good dope on them.

In the evening after he had arranged his notes on the captured nannies and recorded them, he studied his detailed map, trying to figure out how to get up to the areas where he had seen the billies from time to time. They were never together, except that sometimes a billy would have one or two yearlings with him, like apprentices learning the ropes from the old man.

He went to bed even earlier than usual so he would wake before dawn. An early start would help. He couldn't climb till it was light, but he could get all his preparations made and then take off as soon as the sun came up. He had a route in mind that was going to be very tough climbing, but it would get him up high where maybe he could watch a billy or two from above.

He was relieved, when his alarm clock went off in the dark, to find that it was not raining. It was cold, though. He packed his backpack carefully. He might be out all day. The trail he had in mind was a long one, and he needed a lot of gear. His camera equipment, his binoculars, and the high-powered scope, his notebook and pencils, an extra sweater, food, a knife. I look like a Boy Scout's dream of himself, he thought. He gave up the idea of taking a thermos of coffee. It would go good, up on those high peaks, but it was one more bulky thing to carry. He'd make do with melting water. You had to be careful with that though, too much could cause stomach cramps and that was no fun at all. He'd done it lots of times when he'd been hot and the water tasted good.

He heaved the pack onto his shoulders, fastened the straps, and straightened up. In his hand he took his favorite climbing stick, one he made himself last winter, a sturdy stick with an iron hook in one end of it. It was useful sometimes on the rock faces. He had his rope looped and hung over his shoulder.

"*Hasta la vista*," he said to a chipmunk who peered at him curiously. "Here goes the walking research lab. See ya in church."

For some distance he walked along gently sloping land that gradually became more rugged. He was heading for the mountains around Beaver Woman Lake. There were only unimproved trails going in there, and it was not a place where even the more ambitious climbers usually went. Therefore, he hoped, it would be good goat country.

When he got to the lake at last, he went out on a little point of gravel that was covered with brush already turning to fall colors. He eased out of his pack and sat down heavily. Tired already, and he hadn't begun the difficult part of the climb. The sun beat down on his head, but the shadows were icy cold. He decided he liked the sun better. In a few minutes he struggled to his feet and lay on his stomach at the water's edge, splashing his head and neck and arms with the nearly freezing water. He knelt and drank slowly.

There were fishlike green shadows moving about in the lake. Near to the bank, a fish—a silver salmon he'd guess from her size and shape—was clearing a place beneath an overhang of river rock. Back and forth she swam, moving slowly and using her tail like a whisk broom, clearing away rotted leaves and small stones until she had a space about five inches in diameter cleared and ready for her eggs. Nearby and poking his inquisitive nose into the nest from time to time swam the protective male waiting to fertilize the eggs and start new life.

Fantastic life cycle, the salmon, thought Gordon. In spite of all the studies done on them, no one really understood why they migrated to the sea and then returned against overwhelming odds to the mountain lakes where they began the cycle again.

He got out his notebook and made notes on the lake, and the general terrain. On the other side of the lake, where he meant to start the climb, conifers grew down near the shore and straggled for a little distance up the path of the gulch. The butte that he had to climb reared up into the sky like an ancient, unfinished castle.

Better eat before he left. He chewed absently, staring at the face of the butte, studying it through glasses, looking for the best way up. At first he could circle the base, going up gradually, but eventually the only thing to do was dig in and climb. He squinted at the thing, looking for crags and crevices, until he had a kind of map of the butte fixed in his mind.

When he had finished his lunch, he set up his scope on its folding tripod and scanned the peaks that surrounded the butte.

"Ha!" he said. "Jackpot." Way up on a ledge, a billy goat stood staring into space; and still further up and around toward the west, a billy and a yearling, standing some distance apart from the other, grazed. "What I've got to do," Gordon said aloud, "is to get up on that peak behind and above them, without their seeing me." He set up his camera with the telephoto lens and took some pictures, but what he really wanted to do was to get close enough to see the goats clearly with the naked eye. As Mr. Rankin was fond of saying, there's no substitute for the good old naked eye.

He got his gear together, hoisted up the backpack, and set out. When he came around to the other side of the lake, he picked out a place where he could stash some of the gear. It would be too hard to make the climb with everything. His food he wrapped in a waterproof cover and left swinging from a branch of a fir tree out of the reach of any animal that might get interested in it.

The scope and the tripod in their cases would be

all right leaning up against a tree, and so would the pack itself with the hatchet, extra sweater, Scout knife, plastic sheet, and the small first aid kit. He slung the camera strap over his shoulder, the binoculars around his neck, and at the last minute decided to tie his sweater around his waist. It could get cold without warning, up that high. He put one foil-wrapped sandwich inside his shirt front. It would get mashed probably but it was well-wrapped and would taste good after that strenuous climb.

At first it was fairly easy climbing. He followed a game trail for a way, and then hoisted himself up from one heavy overhang to another. After that the climbing suddenly got much harder. There were small waterfalls, or not real waterfalls but sheets of water spilling out over the rocks, making them slippery and hard to climb. He tried to stay in the folds of the cliff. His observer's eye noted the varied colors of the rocks in the folds—mostly red, but some yellow, some white, even a few shades of green. It would be great to know what kinds of rocks they were, and he made a mental note to ask Mr. Rankin about them.

Then the climbing got so rough that he didn't notice anything except the surface right before him. He unbuckled his climbing stick with one hand and used it twice to help himself from one ledge up to another, but the third time the hook on the end of the stick bit into a pocket of rubble that came loose with such a jerk Gordon had to drop the stick to keep from falling. He heard it go banging and clattering down the cliffside. It took a couple of minutes of just standing still to get his nerve back. If a guy was going to do this kind of climbing, he ought to go to mountain-climbing school. He ought to have pitons and all that. But this was no time to think about that. He looked up and picked out his next hold. Carefully he pulled himself up, testing everything first.

It seemed like half a lifetime before he finally reached the spot he had been aiming at. It was not as level as it had looked from down below, but there was room for him to stretch out anyway. He lay flat on his back and tried to get his breathing back to normal and his muscles to stop their jerking. He'd made it.

12

THE sun was low in the sky, but it felt warm
and the sky was almost cloudless. Gordon felt a
strong temptation just to lie still and doze a little.
The sudden relaxation, after the tension of the
climb, and the thin air, and the fact that he had
been on the move since before dawn all combined
to make him feel very sleepy.

But that kind of thinking led nowhere. "You
didn't come up here for the sunbathing, Mohlen,"
he said. Talking to himself again! He wondered
if everybody did who was alone for a long period of
time.

Pulling out the binoculars, he looked them over
carefully. They had a couple of knocks against the
rocks on his way up, but they seemed to be all right.
He held them to his eyes and looked toward the
adjacent peak, where he had seen two billies and
the yearling.

He gasped. The billy who was with the yearling was very close. They could both be clearly seen without glasses. Both were a little below him, the yearling on a ledge just under the billy, standing there like statues, looking away from Gordon.

He put down the glasses and got the pencil and pad from his pocket. Squinting with one eye, he guessed at their measurements and weight. The billy looked like an old fellow: he was thick-set and his coat had a pale yellow cast. Gordon guessed he weighed around three hundred pounds. Maybe six feet from nose to tail. The great curved sweep of shiny black horns was beautiful. With the glasses he could make out at least twelve rings. That meant the old boy was over twelve years old. From what Gordon had read, he knew that goats sometimes lived to be fourteen or fifteen, but this was a grand-daddy, all right. His beard and his long coat were blowing in the thermal winds that were already beginning their descent, swirling and eddying around the peaks.

The yearling was perhaps half the old goat's size, but he stood with the same stolid self-assurance as the older goat.

Gordon looked for the other billy he had seen from the lake, and eventually spotted him, a little further away and rather hard to see because he was on an overhang that was directly below Gordon. He didn't seem to be as big as the other billy. Gordon held his glasses with one hand and tried to

sketch the goat with the other. Along with mountain climbing, he thought, I need a course in art. But he got a pretty good impression of him down, after all.

The other two, when Gordon turned his attention back to them, still stood ignoring each other. Gordon lay on his stomach with his chin propped on his arms, watching. Then, on what seemed a sudden impulse, the yearling made two downward jumps, with the slow, effortless grace of a hang-glider. Gordon could just see the top of his head and his horns after he landed on his new perch. The old billy showed no sign at all of having noticed the yearling's move. Surely he wouldn't continue to stand motionless on that tiny ledge after darkness came!

Gordon found himself staying almost as still as the goat. He studied everything about him that he could see, trying to fix it all in his memory. It would be a real coup to get that older goat into his trap, but he knew he didn't have a chance of that. The old fellow wouldn't come down far enough, for one thing. And for another, he would be far too cautious. So any statistics he prepared would just have to be based on estimate.

He noticed that the tip of one horn was broken. It might just have worn down over the years, or the goat may have been in a fight, or perhaps the horns just began to wear down with age. He knew from what he had read that billy goats sometimes got ornery during the mating season and might thrash around in bushes and against rocks with their horns, and sometimes even fight each other, though usually not very seriously.

The goat lifted his head. Gordon looked up, too.

He couldn't see anything, but in a minute he heard the whirr of a helicopter, and then he saw it, heading off toward the general area of Gunsight Lake. Maybe just looking for forest fires.

For the first time since he had reached the summit, Gordon looked far down at the valley. He was startled to see it was dark down there, although up on his peak there was still bright sunlight. He watched the darkness fill up the valleys like a river, slowly flooding the sides of the mountains with darkness. It was strange to see night come from beneath instead of closing in overhead. He supposed he ought to start down, but he wanted to wait and see what the goat was going to do. Surely he wouldn't stand there all night. What did he do when darkness came? Common sense told Gordon to get started, but this was a chance in a million. And after all, it wasn't going to take all that long to go down the mountain. It wasn't like coming up. He took the sandwich out of his shirt, unwrapped it, and ate it. He was thirsty, but there was no water at hand, so he would have to stay dry a little while.

He took a lot of pictures of the goat, trying to get at him from different angles, although there wasn't much choice, with the goat unmoving against the rock like an ancient petroglyph.

He shifted his position a little and started a small slide of loose rock. All three of the goats heard it. The loner on the ledge jumped up to a ledge where Gordon could see him even better than before. The old billy goat looked around in a leisurely way, saw Gordon, stared at him thoughtfully for a few seconds, then braced his feet on the rock wall and boosted himself up to the next ledge. He was now above Gordon, but he didn't seem to be especially concerned.

I ought to start down, Gordon thought. I've got a long way to go. But if he waited a little longer, he might get to see where the goats spent the night, and besides, everything was so beautiful. The sky was no longer streaked with the colors of sunset but had darkened to pure midnight blue that seemed to glow as if some strange sun were burning behind it. The old familiar sun was falling behind the peaks to the west of him, and it occurred to him that being up where he was made him a part of somebody else's sunset.

There was still enough light to photograph the old goat, and he got some very good shots of the yearling. The young goat seemed more restless than the old one, possibly more worried about Gordon. In about fifteen minutes he began a series of upward jumps that took him out of sight.

There must be, Gordon thought, some level place,

possibly some very high alpine meadow, where they went. He wanted very much to see it. The habits of the solitary billies seemed to be quite different from the nannies, at least in the summer. He felt that his report wouldn't be complete if he didn't get the whole story.

The sunlight on the peak where he sat was bright, and it was eerie to watch night filling in the final hollows of the earth while he sat up there, brightly lit. "Like a god of the mountain," he said aloud, and chuckled. "Gordon Mohlan, god of the mountain." The wind tossed his words away, and probably not even the old goat heard him. That's just as well, he thought: people that go around claiming to be gods are apt to get smacked down. He looked up at the clear sky, and then around at the magnificent mountain range. No wonder the Indians thought up gods for all the different forces of nature. You could really get to thinking that way, if you lived in places like this. God of the sun, god of the moon, god of thunder. . . .

As if to reenforce his thought, a long, jagged flash of lightning cut across the lower, darker mountains to the east. He glanced at the sky again. Didn't look like much chance of a storm here, though you could never tell, of course.

Thunder rumbled in the distance. The old billy goat stirred himself, shaking his head a little like an old man jolted out of his daydreaming. Then with the same easy grace that the yearling had shown, he sailed upward and disappeared.

"Darn it!" Gordon said aloud. "They look like they're not going to move a muscle for a hundred years, and then while you blink an eye, they're gone."

The jump had taken the goat off to Gordon's left, and Gordon decided that if he could ease himself along his narrow ledge, let himself down a little to the next ledge, maybe he could see them.

There was no way he could get above them without going down and climbing an altogether different peak, and there was no time for that today, nor did he have the energy left. So ease over there real careful, boy—watch it—let yourself down little by little. Easy does it. It wasn't a very wide ledge but it would hold him. I'm getting to be a doggone goat, he said to himself.

It worked. Although he had moved down, and the goats had climbed up, he had come to a point of vantage where he could see right into the tiny meadow where they were. Both the kid and the old billy were there, chomping away on what little grass there was. They weren't very near, but with the glasses he could see them clearly. The yearling was eating lichen off a rock face, and the old billy was nibbling away at a spot of mountain sorrel.

Poor old goats. It wasn't easy scratching out an existence at these altitudes. When he got home, Gordon thought, the first thing he was going to do was ride his bike to MacDonald's and order three

84

Big Macs, and a chocolate shake. And fries. And onion rings. Obviously, he was hungry. Well, pretty soon he would go down to the lake and camp there for the night, and go on back to the chalet in the morning.

Meanwhile, across the way, the billy goat stalked past the yearling as if the younger goat didn't exist and began to feed in another corner of the tiny meadow. Gordon wondered if the yearling got on the old boy's nerves. Invasion of privacy. But there was no attempt to drive the young one off, and the old one certainly could if he took a mind to. Gordon put a new roll of film into his camera and got some pretty good shots of both goats. He was also making notes in his notebook.

Perhaps because he had been so absorbed, he hadn't noticed the change in the sky. But a sudden smash of thunder made him look up. He was no longer the god of the sunlit peaks. He was a humble human being clinging to a precarious perch on a butte with rain descending in a torrent. Lightning played from peak to peak, and the thunder was almost continuous.

He was frightened, but he was a lot safer from lightning on the ledge than he would have been on top of the butte. All he could do was huddle close to the rock, trying, like the goats, to stay out of the rain. He unwound the sleeves of his sweater from around his waist and covered his head with it. He could smell the wet wool; and in a few minutes the

85

sweater was a soggy mass. He squeezed it out and put it behind his back. At least it made a tiny pad of comfort between him and the cold rock.

He could see nothing at all through the sheets of rain, let alone his goats. No doubt they had found whatever shelter they could. He winced as a shaft of lightning flashed very close, and flattened himself still more against the dark, streaming rock. The noise of the wind and the thunder was deafening.

He clenched his hands on rocks until his fingers ached, as a series of small landslides began in the mud around him. Rocks, rubble, dirt, and chunks of snow began to slide and rattle, coming down from above his head.

"What am I doing here?" he yelled into the wind, thinking again of his cousin working in the quiet bank, doing sensible things. And yet he wouldn't swap places for anything, not even now.

The storm lasted for some time. By the time it stopped, Gordon was so wet, so cold, so frightened that he couldn't even think any longer. He could only cling to his precarious shelter and wait.

Like many mountain storms, when it was over, it was over suddenly. The only moisture was the dripping of the collected rainwater from the surfaces above him and the wet on the ground below him. He waited for the sky to lighten, for the moon to come. During the course of the storm, night had reached the mountaintops.

It stayed dark and he began to feel real panic,

for the first time this summer. He couldn't huddle on that narrow ledge all night. Already he was so cramped his muscles were a mass of shooting pains. If he fell asleep he might fall off. In fact, he almost certainly would and he didn't think he could stay awake all night.

It took him a good five minutes to face up to the alternative. He was going to have to climb to the top of the butte and spend the night there. At least there was room enough to stretch out and sleep.

But getting up there in the dark was not his idea of a way to spend a summer evening. He tried the flashlight that hung from his belt. Surprisingly, in spite of the knocks it had gotten on the climb, it still worked. It wasn't his big, powerful flashlight, though: he had left that back at the chalet because it was so bulky and he had expected to be home by dark. Still, it was a light. Very slowly and carefully, he played it over the surface just above him. It wasn't such a long way. If he were a goat, he could easily jump it. But it was very steep, and it was also wet and slippery.

He plotted his route, memorizing very carefully where each protruding rock was, because once he started climbing, he couldn't use the light. He'd need both hands. All right, Mohlen, get up there. He rubbed his hands in some dirt that had fallen onto his ledge, then reached up and felt for the next highest ledge. It was so small, he wouldn't be able to rest on it, just use it as a stepping stone. He looked up at the sky. It was many shades of blue and struck with light. The stars were out.

"God," he said, "would you mind keeping an eye on a foolhardy goat watcher? I was only kidding about being god of the mountain." He grasped the ledge above him and scrambled upward, using his knees much as he had seen the goats do.

He reached at once for the next ledge above him, and hand over hand he sought for holds, praying that slides hadn't weakened his "steps."

Twice he paused for a second, leaning hard into the face of the cold rock, getting his breath, before he tried for the next ledge. His muscles kept cramping with the cold, and that worried him.

At last, after the longest period of time he could ever remember living through, he pulled himself over the top of the butte and lay full length on his stomach, gasping and shivering. He would have to stay here all night, of course, and his food, his blanket—just about everything he really needed— were down by the lake. But never mind, he was here, he was all in one piece. He rolled over on his back and looked up at the stars that seemed so close in the sky.

With chattering teeth, he said, "Thanks, God. That was a good job of search and rescue."

13

THERE was no danger of falling asleep. Not when he was shivering from head to foot, and his teeth were chattering. His sodden sweater was no good to him. He tied the hood of his parka tightly around his neck and sat with his arms wrapped around his knees. The winds came at him like sharp icicles. The quilted nylon parka that was often uncomfortably warm when he was climbing acted as a windbreaker to some degree, but not enough.

He made himself stand up and run in place. That helped a little, but the wind was so strong, he was afraid it would blow him right off the butte. After all, even goats died that way sometimes, and their old suction-cup feet had a much better grasp on rock—on reality—than his Norm Thompson boots, good though they were.

He found a small amount of debris that the storm

had dumped near him, mostly twigs and some wet leaves and, of all things, a gum wrapper, blown in from who knew where. Heaping as much of it together as he could, trying to protect it from the wind, he lit it with his metal match. But even with one arm around the tiny flame to keep the wind off it, all that came of it was a brief flare-up that burned his hand and went out. It had been a silly thing to do. The altitude and the strain and the hunger had made him light-headed. Better get a grip on himself. "Don't ever tell Mr. Rankin you tried to make a fire out of six twigs, twelve wet leaves, and a gum wrapper," he said, trying to cheer himself.

If he had known, he could have portioned out the sandwich, saved part of it for now. That would have helped his hunger. But wasn't hunger just a state of mind? After all, he'd had lunch and breakfast. Still he was hungry just the same. He began to think about the food he liked: steak, chili dogs, lima beans, garlic bread, chili, pancakes with blueberry syrup, pancakes with anything or nothing, hot coffee. For a full minute he fantasized holding a big mug of steaming hot coffee, hot enough to burn his mouth.

To get his mind off food, he concentrated on the goats. What were they doing? Sleeping? Didn't they ever get cold? Of course, they had that nifty fur coat. Did they ever get hungry and want a snack in the middle of the night? Up here there wouldn't be a whole lot to choose from. No toasted peanut butter sandwiches. No cocoa. Only moss and lichens. He wondered what moss and lichens tasted like. Some of those outdoor writers claimed you could eat practically anything, as long as it wasn't poisonous.

With his knife he scraped a fragment of wet lichen off the face of the rock and cautiously tasted it; what was lichen anyway? What had they said in biology? A combination of fungi and algae, wasn't it? Fungus has no chlorophyll of its own so it sets up housekeeping with the algae. Good old symbiosis. He took another very small bite. It wasn't what he'd call a taste thrill. Maybe he wasn't all that hungry, after all.

The wind was bitter. Or winds, really. They seemed to come from all directions, way up on top. He tried to imagine people down in the valley: people eating supper in their campers; people watching television; people at the movies; listening to the stereo with a fire in the fireplace; going over to the A&W for a chili dog; talking. And there he was, Gordon Mohlen, as removed from the world as if he were perched on the point of a distant star with no other human beings on it. It was easier, up here, to feel like one of the goats than it was to feel like a human being. Had Grizzly Adams and Jim Bridger and those old-time mountain men who went months without seeing another person felt the same? Had they sometimes thought of themselves as a bear or an antelope or something?

Below him a thick bank of cloud had moved in, and more than ever he felt himself a dweller of the sky, cut off from the earth. Above his head, so close it seemed as though he could pull them down around him, the stars blazed with light. In spite of his physical discomforts, he felt exalted. He would not have missed this for anything.

Whether the winds dropped some of their force or he simply grew used to them, he began to feel less cold. He even slept for a little while, although he had not expected to. His sweater dried out enough to give him some added protection against the cold when he wrapped it around his shoulders outside the parka.

When the sky began to turn gray, he saw the dim figure of one of the goats appear on the opposite cliff. At first it was hard to tell if it was the big billy himself or not, but he seemed big enough. And then as the sun came up, Gordon saw that it was. The goat looked directly at him, as he had the day before, but he seemed neither alarmed nor curious. After a long stare, he found some moss and began his breakfast.

"You ought to be more careful," Gordon told him, his words again tossed away in the wind. "Sometimes, you know, a guy will shoot at a feller like you, some stupid guy with a scope on his rifle, just for the fun of seeing you fall off. Some guys have a very weird sense of humor. Yeah, I know, this is the Park and hunting isn't allowed, but you watch it, just the same. People break the rules, you know. So you be a little more careful, you hear?" But of course the old billy goat wouldn't be more careful. He didn't get shot at often enough to learn caution. Anyway, what could he really do to be careful? A goat on a ledge was a sitting duck, but that was where he lived.

Gordon watched the sunrise and thought he had never seen one so beautiful. There was still a belt of cloud below him, although it was beginning to thin as the sun came up. The warmth and light of the sun were like a blessing. Over his head a golden eagle circled slowly. In spite of hunger and stiffness and cold, Gordon suddenly didn't want to leave. But of course he had to. Common sense and all that. He was not, after all, a goat. Nor an eagle, either.

He stretched his arms and legs to get the stiffness out, took one long last look at the old billy, and started down the side of the mountain.

When he got to the lake, he built up a good fire on the coarse sand, retrieved his pack from the tree, and had breakfast. It had been a night he would never forget in all his life.

14

THE nanny picked her way expertly across the treacherous loose rock, her kid close behind her. Winter was in the air. Already snow had fallen in the high places. The nanny was looking for a protected spot on the southern side of the mountain. Later, if the snow piled up too much, she would move again, higher, to a place where the winds kept the mountain scrubbed clean of snow. In the past year she had travelled about fifteen miles.

The other nannies were moving too, but they no longer stayed in such a tight little band. Each one, with her kid if she had one, sought her own place. In about two months the breeding season would begin, and when the new kids were born in late spring, the ones who were now with their mothers would be encouraged or forced to go out on their own, perhaps tagging along with a billy.

The nanny jumped up into a cleft in the rock worn by water and wind, and plodded along, her head down. After a while she came to a dead end in the narrow gulch. Above her was sheer perpendicular rock, with no ledges, no footholds at all. She considered for a moment, then reared up on her hind legs and pivotted around to start back. There wasn't room for her to pass the kid, so she pushed him with her nose to turn him back. He didn't like being in the lead, but he had no choice. Every few minutes he stopped to look back at her uncertainly. When the trail finally widened out enough so that she could pass him, he settled into a contented shuffle behind her.

She headed off in a slightly different direction, now climbing, now leaping. A game trail led finally in an upward and southerly direction. It was very narrow, with rock cliff on one side, a long drop on the other, but she walked it without hurry and without hesitation.

Then at a sharp bend in the trail, she found herself face to face with Gordon. They both stopped. Actually, neither had a choice.

"So there you are," he said. "I've been hunting all over for you, like five or six days. I have to move out tomorrow, have to go on home. I wanted to say so long. I haven't got a collar on you, but you know what? I'm kind of glad I haven't. Except that this fall and winter when I fly up here in the Forest Service plane . . . *if* I do . . . I'll know where every-

body is but you. But that's all right. You're en-
titled to your privacy."

She pawed the trail impatiently.

"Wait. I'll back off in a sec. I wanted to tell you
I went up to where I guess you go in winter. I saw
this big old billy. For all I know, he may be your
mate. Listen, I really liked it up there. I mean I
really kind of found out what being a goat is all
about, I think. Well, a little bit."

The nanny pawed the ground again and tossed
her head.

"All right." He took a step back. "Hey, I took
down the pen in case you want to use that salt lick
again. There was a porky living in it, and he was
mad as heck when I turned him out. But that's the
way it goes." He took another step backward.

The goat tensed and turned her head.

"What is it?"

She pushed her kid against the overhanging rock
and pulled in against it herself, looking up.

An avalanche of rock and gravel and snow shot
out of the cliff above them and cascaded down the
mountain. Gordon watched the heavy mass rocket
past him. He hadn't heard it at all until it was almost upon them, but the goat had heard it. He
thanked his lucky star that he had been under the
overhang.

When he was sure it was over, he flattened his
hands against the rock and listened for the landslide
further down the mountain. All he heard was the

wind and the rattle of a few pebbles and water dripping. He moved back as far as he could so the
nanny could get by him. "Thanks for everything,"
he said.

She ignored him. Calm and unperturbed she
picked her way around the cliff.

"Have a good winter," he called after her.
"Good-bye for now."

She didn't look back.

15

THE mountain goat stood on a rocky ledge, far up in the mountains. A swirl of snow danced around her head. At some distance from her, the kid cautiously explored a steep incline, making his own decisions about where to put his feet. The long winter hair had begun to grow in, making both goats look bigger and bulkier than they had during the summer. A sound, either thunder or a landslide somewhere in the distance, made them look up.

Still higher, a billy goat hunched his shoulders against the wind and the snow and stared at the world. In another two months he or some other billy would pick his way down from his lofty peak and seek out the nanny. Perhaps there would be more than one billy, and there would be some threats and some tough posturing between the billies until one gave way to the other. It was unlikely that they would actually fight.

Toward the end of December the breeding season would be over, and the billies would once more go their solitary ways. Some time between May and June there would be a baby kid born, or even a pair of twins. Then the kid who now remained with his mother would be left to his own devices, a yearling, almost an adult.

The sun came out, very pale in the white sky, showing through the whirlwind of snow. And gradually the snow stopped falling. But the short summer of the northern Rockies was over. Down at the lower altitudes there would be the transition time of autumn, but here it was already winter. The goat turned away from her view of the valley far below her. She leaped up to a ledge just big enough for her four feet, and hardly pausing, up again, and began to eat the lichen that clung to the rocks.

The Mountain Goat

Oreamnos Americanus: also called mountain goat, Rocky Mountain goat, white goat.

Family: bovidae (which includes cattle, sheep, goats). Distantly related to Old World antelopes, including the European chamois.

Origins: probably Asia. May have crossed to America over the Bering Land Bridge, 600,000 years ago.

Habitat: high mountains, cliffs, in the western areas of North America, from Alaska and Yukon to Montana, Idaho, Washington.

Physical description: beard grows below jaw on both sexes; long hair almost pure white, sometimes tinged with yellow; the only native North American mammal that produces wool; sheds slightly in summer. Coat 3 to 4 inches thick.

WEIGHT: 125 to 300 pounds, males usually heavier than females.

HEIGHT: from shoulder, 3 to 3½ feet.

LENGTH: just under 5 feet to 5¾.

HORNS: grow continually, curving slightly backward. Male's horns may reach 1 foot in length, female's 9 inches. Horns are black, hollow, brittle. Annual growth rings show age of goat. Kid's horns start as two small buttons, which grow to 3 inches by the first winter, reach 5 or 6 inches by the age of 16 months.

HOOVES: adult male front hoof almost square, about 2½ inches across, hind foot slightly smaller. Female's are smaller. Pad is convex, of spongy material that acts as suction cup.

SEX GLAND: both sexes have crescent-shaped gland in back of each horn, which, in the male, becomes enlarged and gives off waxy substance in breeding season.

Range: possibly 100 to 200 acres in the summer; more restricted and higher in winter. Perhaps 15 to 20 miles travelled in a year.

Breeding season: November, December. Females breed at 2½ years.

Gestation period: 178 days.

Kids: usually 7 to 8 pounds, slightly over 2 feet tall at shoulder. Usually one kid, occasionally twins. Able to stand and jump almost at once. Weaned at 6 to 8 weeks, but eats vegetation after a few days.

Life span: 12 to 15 years.

Enemies: mountain lions, bears, wolves, man, parasites (tapeworms and ticks). Eagles may capture young kids.

Food: lichens, moss, mountain sorrel, green vegetation. Has a four-chambered stomach, chews its cud. Has no teeth on top jaw in front, has 32 teeth: 8 incisors, 12 premolars, 12 molars. Feeding habits are diurnal. Feeds in morning and late afternoon.

Bibliography

Audubon Nature Encyclopedia, Vol. 4, Curtis Publishing Company, New York, 1965.

BANSNER, URSULA, *Mountain Goat–Human Interactions*, Univ. of Montana, summarized in *Hungry Horse News*, Columbia Falls, Montana, August 14, 1975.

CHADWICK, DOUGLAS, Master's thesis on mountain goats, University of Montana, 1974.

FIELD MUSEUM OF NATURAL HISTORY, Zoological Series, Volume 3, 1900–04, Chicago, Illinois, June 1900.

Hammond Nature Atlas of America, A Ridge Press Book, Hammond Inc., Maplewood, N.J., 1975.

Hungry Horse News, Columbia Falls, Montana. June 13, 1975, July 31, 1975, August 14, 1975, August 21, 1975.

MACLEAN, GORDON, Hamilton, Montana, interviewed in *The Missoulian*, Missoula, Montana, June 4, 1972.

The Missoulian, Missoula, Montana, June 4, 1972, November 30, 1974.

The New Hunters' Encyclopedia, 3rd revised edition, Stackpole Publishing Company, Harrisburg, Pa., 1966.

RIDEOUT, CHESTER, University of Kansas, interviewed in *The Missoulian*, Missoula, Montana, June 4, 1972.

RUE, LEONARD LEE, III, *Game Animals*, Harper and Row, New York, 1968.

WISTER, OWEN, "The White Goat and His Ways," from *Musk-Ox, Bison, Sheep and Goats*, the American Sportsman's Library, edited by Caspar Whitney, George Bird Grinnell, and Owen Wister, Macmillan Company, New York, 1904.

	DATE DUE	